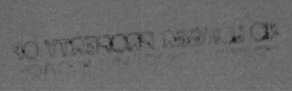

Baby Blessings

To all parents of the world. For we are given an abundance of blessings with the birth of a child.
May we pour our love into the blessings of our children.
Then he took the children in his arms and placed his hands on their heads and blessed them.
Bless this new life, bless each day, as you bless this family.
—D. J.

To my sister, Pat, and her two grandsons, B. B. and Zion
—J. E. R.

SIMON & SCHUSTER BOOKS FOR YOUNG READERS
An imprint of Simon & Schuster Children's Publishing Division
1230 Avenue of the Americas, New York, New York 10020
Text copyright © 2010 by Deloris Jordan
Illustrations copyright © 2010 by James E. Ransome
All rights reserved, including the right of reproduction in whole or in part in any form.
SIMON & SCHUSTER BOOKS FOR YOUNG READERS is a trademark of Simon & Schuster, Inc.
For information about special discounts for bulk purchases, please contact
Simon & Schuster Special Sales at 1-866-506-1949 or business@simonandschuster.com.
The Simon & Schuster Speakers Bureau can bring authors to your live event.
For more information or to book an event,
contact the Simon & Schuster Speakers Bureau at
1-866-248-3049 or visit our website at www.simonspeakers.com.

Book design by Laurent Linn
The text for this book is set in Paradigm.
The illustrations for this book are rendered in oil paints.
Manufactured in China
2 4 6 8 10 9 7 5 3 1
Library of Congress Cataloging-in-Publication Data
Jordan, Deloris.
Baby blessings : a prayer for the day you are born / Deloris Jordan ; illustrated by James Ransome.
— 1st ed.
p. cm.
"A Paula Wiseman book."
ISBN 978-1-4169-5362-3 (hardcover)
1. Children—Prayers and devotions. I. Ransome, James. II. Title.
BL625.5.J67 2010
242'.62—dc22
2008017131

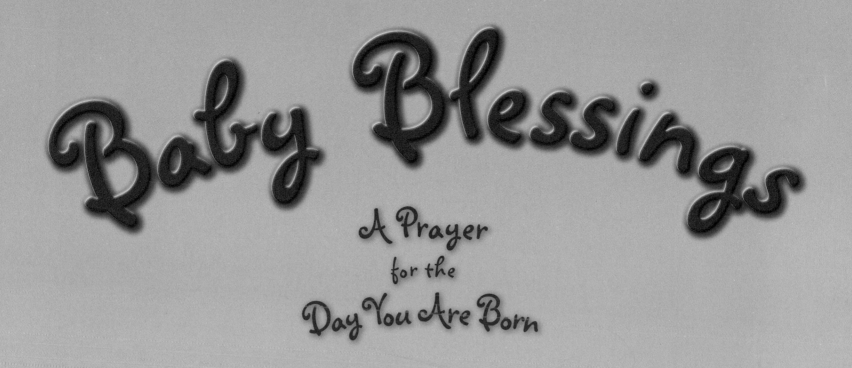

Baby Blessings

A Prayer
for the
Day You Are Born

DELORIS JORDAN

illustrated by **JAMES E. RANSOME**

—• A PAULA WISEMAN BOOK •—

SIMON & SCHUSTER BOOKS FOR YOUNG READERS

—• NEW YORK   LONDON   TORONTO   SYDNEY •—

Today you are born.

You will always be loved
with a love that knows no bounds.

You will touch the world
in your own special way.

We pray that you will always be kind.

Remember to always believe in yourself.

Always strive to do your best.

Remember to look for
the good in every day.

We will always be there,
ready to listen to your dreams
and visions, ready to guide you.

We will always stand by you.

Believe and trust in God
and his promises of blessings.

Our dear child, you will
always be rewarded with love.

You will be showered with many blessings along the way.

It can and will come true.

You are our beloved child.

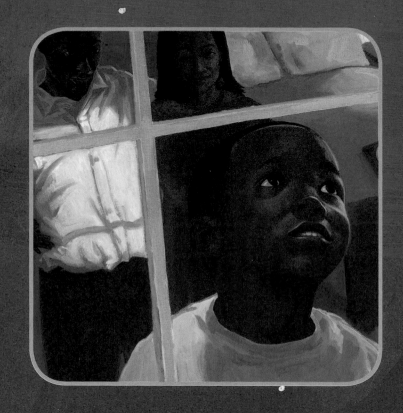

We are blessed.